About the Author

A scientific report writer and a mum of two children. Inspired to write in the early hours when the insomnia prevails.

Bertie's and Freda's Adventures: In Search of the Sea

JFF Barretto

Bertie's and Freda's Adventures: In Search of the Sea

Olympia Publishers
London

www.olympiapublishers.com
OLYMPIA PAPERBACK EDITION

A CIP catalogue record for this title is
available from the British Library.

ISBN: 978-1-78830-616-4

This is a work of fiction.
Names, characters, places and incidents originate from the writer's
imagination. Any resemblance to actual persons, living or dead, is
purely coincidental.

First Published in 2020

Olympia Publishers
Tallis House
2 Tallis Street
London
EC4Y 0AB

Printed in Great Britain

Dedication

For Alicia and Sebastian, my inspiration and Craig for the support.

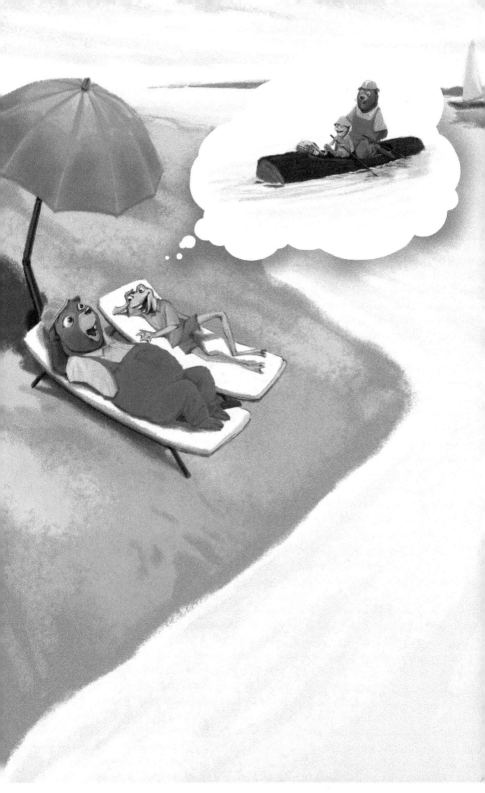

Bertie beaver was resting by the river one day when Freda frog hopped his way.

"Hello," said Freda, "How are you?"

"I'm fine," replied Bertie, "How do you do?"

"Please will you help build a boat with me? I'd like to have an adventure and sail upon the sea."

Bertie smiled and then replied, "I will help you, but only if I can come too."

Freda hopped and leapt until she found the right tree and shouted to Bertie, "Come over and see."

With a chomp, chomp, chomp and a stomp, stomp, stomp Bertie worked his way around and the tree slowly tumbled to the ground.

With a gnaw, gnaw, gnaw and a bang, bang, bang, with a ribbit, ribbit, ribbit and a clang, clang, clang the boat was finally done.

Freda and Bertie launched their boat in the shining
sun.

With a row, row, row and a splash, splash, splash
they glided down the river with smiles.

But they soon faded, when they came across some hungry crocodiles.

"Hello," said the crocodiles, "Come and join us for some tea?"

"No thank you," said Freda "We really can't stop, we're off to find the sea."

With a row, row, row and a splash, splash, splash they paddled as fast as they could.

But came to a stop when they hit some mice, adrift on a piece of wood.

"Hello," squeaked the mice, "We're stuck on this bark, do you think can you help us three? We were sitting on a branch, when it broke off as a beaver chomped down our tree."

"Oh dear!" sighed Bertie, "Come aboard, we're off to find the sea."

With a row, row, row and a splash, splash, splash along the water the boat sped.

But it slowed down when berries kept landing on top of Bertie's head.

"Hello," said the cheeky monkeys laughing in the trees, "Come hang and play with us."

"No thank you," said Freda, "We can't stop, we must find the sea before dusk."

With a row, row, row and a splash, splash, splash the boat sped along again.

But came to a stop as a herd of elephants were seen
wading round the bend.

"Hello," said the elephants, "Come stay and bathe
with us today."

"No thank you," said Freda "It's getting late, we'd
rather be on our way."

"We can help," trumpeted the elephants, "Would you like some extra speed?"

"Thank you," said Freda, "That would be lovely, it's exactly what we need!"

With a trump, trump, trump and a whoosh, whoosh, whoosh the boat sped along in the breeze.

But all of a sudden, the boat hit a rock that made all five of them freeze.

"Oh no," cried the mice.

"Oh dear," shouted Freda, as the boat bumped from rock to rock.

"Oh no, oh dear," Bertie cried out, they were all in a state of shock.

With a bump, bump, bump and a swirl, swirl, swirl everyone was getting dizzy going around and around.

When all of a sudden, the river had ended and the boat started to fall down.

Holding tight, the mice shrieked and yelled. Freda and Bertie got ready to jump.

But all the boat did was land in the deep blue sea
with a great big **THUMP!**

"What's next?" the mice enquired, as Freda brought out a map.

"I'll tell you all in a while, my friends," she said, "But first let's take a nap."

Bertie and the mice closed their eyes, wondering what their next adventure would be.

Freda had a good idea as she could hear murmurings coming from under the sea.

CPSIA information can be obtained
at www.ICGtesting.com
Printed in the USA
BVHW020155210720
584220BV00019B/470

9 781788 306164